Pen, Penny, Tuppence

Pen, Penny, Tuppence

BARBARA SLEIGH

Illustrated by
MEG STEVENS

HAMISH HAMILTON

LONDON

First published in Great Britain 1968
by Hamish Hamilton Ltd.,
90 Great Russell Street, London, W.C.1

SBN: 241 91359 4

Reproduced by photo-lithography and made at the Pitman Press, Bath

Penny was six years old. Sometimes she was called Pen. When her father was pleased with her he called her Tuppence. When she was naughty he called her by her full name, which was Penelope.

Penny had freckles on her nose and hair that would keep coming loose from the blue ribbon that tied it up at the back, and she liked pretending things because Baby Tim was too little to play games.

"Be quick and wash your hands, Pen," her mother said one day when Penny came home from school. "Cream buns today, because Daddy's home early. He's got something special to tell you."

Penny often took rather a long time to wash. She liked to float her plastic ducks in the basin. Sometimes she dressed the hot tap in her red face-cloth and pretended it was a King sitting on his throne. The cold tap was the Queen with Baby Tim's green face-cloth round it. She talked to the King and Queen in her grandest voice and told them all her secrets. Lately it was always about the puppy she was going to have for her birthday. Today she was as quick as she could be. She just said to the King and Queen:

"I'll tell you all about it later, your Majesties!" She knew that is how you talk to Kings and Queens. Then she ran downstairs.

"Hallo Daddy!" she said as she scrambled up on to her seat. "I wish you came home to tea every day."

Baby Tim was already sitting in his high chair. He was munching a rusk.

"Hallo Tuppence!" said her father. So Penny knew it was a nice "something special" he had to tell.

"Tea first and then surprises!" said her mother.

Penny was dying to hear what the surprise was. When she had caught the last crumb of cream bun with the tip of her tongue from the corner of her mouth, her father said:

"Now for the surprise, Pen. I've got a new job, and we shall be going to live in a new house."

"A new house! How exciting!" said Penny. "Will it be far from here?"

"Quite a long way," said her father, "in the middle of a big town."

Now Penny had lived in the same

house ever since she could remember.
It was not quite in the country, but near
the edge of a housing estate. Sometimes
they all went for picnics in the woods
beyond. She could see the trees over the
rooftops when she looked out of her
bedroom window. She shared the
bedroom with Baby Tim. There was

only just room for his cot and her bed side by side. Penny's dolls all had to live in a box on the landing.

"I shall still be able to have my birthday puppy in the new house, won't I?" asked Penny anxiously.

Her mother looked at her father, and her father looked at her mother, and then her mother said:

"I'm sorry, Pen dear. When we promised, we didn't know about the move. I think we shall have to wait and

see what sort of house Daddy can find. It may not be suitable for a dog."

"Well, if I can't have my puppy I don't want to move!" said Penny crossly. She screwed up her face to keep the tears back. "I hate the new house! I hate it!"

"Penelope!" said her father in a cross voice.

Luckily at that moment Baby Tim's rusk went down the wrong way. He coughed and choked and went red in the face; and he had to be picked up and loved, and patted on the back. While this was going on, Penny slipped off her chair. She went up to the bathroom and told the King and Queen all about it.

"And I don't want a new house if I can't have my puppy!" she said.

The King and Queen didn't say
anything, of course, but the Queen
dripped slow drops of cold water, just
as though she was crying too. This
made Penny feel better.

She could not go on hating the idea of the new house, although she tried. It was too exciting. One Saturday evening her father came home and said:

"Oh dear, I am tired. But I think I've found it!"

"Not the new house we're going to live in?" asked Penny.

Her father nodded. "Three rooms upstairs and two down."

"Oh John, I'm so glad!" said her mother. "Is it sunny?"

"Faces south," said her father.

"And near the shops?"

"Just round the corner!"

"And a school for Penny somewhere near?"

"Five minutes' walk away, next door to a park. Well, young Pen, haven't you anything to ask?"

Penny did not dare to ask the one thing she wanted to know most of all, in case the answer was No.

"Has it got a garden?"

"A tiny one," said her father.

"Then is it—is it a puppy sort of house?"

Her father laughed and nodded.

"Then can I have my puppy for my birthday after all?" said Penny.

"I don't think it would be kind to the puppy to have him before we move. We should have no time to look after him properly," said her father.

"But Daddy—!" began Penny.

"Don't bother Daddy now, Pen dear," said her mother. "Don't you see how tired he is?"

Penny looked at her father. He did look very tired. So this time she

swallowed her tears and went and
fetched his slippers.

"Thank you, Tuppence," he said, and
put them on. Then he lifted her on to
his knee.

"I know how much you want a puppy, old lady," he said. "I promise you shall have one. But you will just have to be patient for a bit. Suppose we say you shall have him as soon as Spring is here—if you are good, and don't keep bothering me about it."

"I promise I won't bother!" said Penny. "And I will try to be good. But, Daddy, how shall I know when Spring has really come?"

"Suppose we say when you hear the cuckoo!" he said.

Penny remembered hearing the cuckoo last year calling: "Cuckoo! Cuckoo!" from the woods in the distance.

"But there is one thing I can promise you as soon as we reach the new house," went on her father.

"Oh, what?" asked Penny.

"A bedroom, all to yourself."

"Not share with Timmy any more?"

"He can have his own room too, next to yours. They will both have to be re-decorated. Would you like to choose your own wallpaper, Pen?"

"Oh, yes!" said Penny. "But, Daddy. Please, are there taps in the new bathroom?"

"Of course there are, Tuppence!

What a funny thing to ask. Now, bring me my pipe and my tobacco, there's a good girl."

Penny slipped off her father's knee and fetched his pipe and his tobacco. Then she ran upstairs to the bathroom and told the King and Queen all about the new house, and the bedroom to herself, and the wallpaper she was going to choose.

"And when the cuckoo comes I shall really and truly have my puppy. He'll be brown, with floppy paws, and I shall call him Bounce," said Penny.

Then she hung the red face-cloth and the green face-cloth back on the sponge-rack, and the King and Queen became just the hot and cold taps again.

Penny chose a pale blue wallpaper with a pattern of tiny white daisies.

"When are we moving to the new house, Daddy?" asked Penny.

"On the day after your birthday," he said.

It was a very queer birthday when it came. Most of the curtains were down, and all the carpets had gone to be cleaned. It made the house all echoey. Nearly all the furniture had gone already. It looked quite lost standing on the pavement waiting to go into the big van.

There was no table to eat Penny's birthday tea on, but her birthday cake stood proudly in the middle of a big packing case. The flames of the seven candles on top of the cake danced just as gaily as if it stood on the grandest shiny table. Penny's mother had taken time off from sewing yards and yards

of new curtains specially to make the
cake. There was bread and butter with
hundreds and thousands sprinkled on
it, too.

"Would you like pink milk or green
milk, Pen?" asked her mother.

"Pink milk, please!" said Penny in
surprise.

Her mother put a drop of the
colouring she used for icing cakes into

Penny's mug of milk. When she stirred it, the milk turned a lovely pale pink. Later on she had a mug of green milk.

Her mother gave her a new pale blue dressing-gown for her new blue bedroom for a birthday present. It had a rabbit on the pocket.

Her father gave her some fluffy blue bedroom slippers to go with the dressing-gown.

Baby Tim only gave her a kiss. It was rather wet but very loving.

"Please may I keep my old dressing-gown for something secret and special?" asked Penny.

"If you like," said her mother. "It's too shabby for Timmy to wear later on."

When Penny went to the bathroom in her new dressing-gown and slippers

she showed them to the King and Queen, and whispered:

"They are lovely, your Majesties, aren't they? But I would much rather have had Bounce than anything. I shall pretend the rabbit on my pocket is a puppy. I didn't say so downstairs in case Daddy thought it was 'bothering'."

It was evening when at last they reached the new house. Penny explored it from top to bottom. She knew which was her bedroom because of the blue wallpaper. It was a dear little room with a cupboard to hang her dresses in.

"I shall sit all my dolls along that shelf," said Penny.

When she looked out of the window she saw how different it was going to be living in the middle of a town. There were roofs and chimneys stretching

away and away, and not a tree to be seen. And there were great tall buildings here and there, full of windows which were just lighting up.

There was one thing which was not a bit different. The taps in the bathroom might have been the same King and

Queen as in the old house, when they were dressed up in the red and green face-cloths.

"I am sorry there aren't any trees, your Majesties," Penny said. "But the great tall buildings shine like fairy palaces when they are all lit up! Now, I've only got to wait until I hear the cuckoo, and then I shall have Bounce."

The days went by, and Penny got

quite used to the new house and her new school. She tried her best to be good, and she did not once bother her father about the puppy.

Snow came and melted away and the days began to grow longer. But she did not hear the cuckoo. Not once.

One day, it was half-term holiday, Baby Tim had a cough.

"I don't want to take him out in this cold wind," said her mother. "Pen dear, do you think you could do some shopping at the Self Service Store for me?"

"Of course I could!" said Penny, feeling very grown-up indeed. "May I spend my pocket-money, too? I've been saving up for something special I saw there."

Her mother nodded. Then she said:

"And you may as well take Daddy's alarm clock to the clock mender's on the way. Daddy was late for work yesterday."

After dinner Penny set off for the shops. She had not far to go. They were on the same side of the road just round the corner. She had her mother's shopping basket with the alarm clock inside in one hand, and she held her mother's purse tightly in the other. It had the shopping list and a ten-shilling note pinned inside for safety.

"Come straight home or I shall get anxious," said her mother.

Penny nodded. She was already pretending that she was a mother with six children at home to shop for, all with measles.

First she went to the clock shop. It

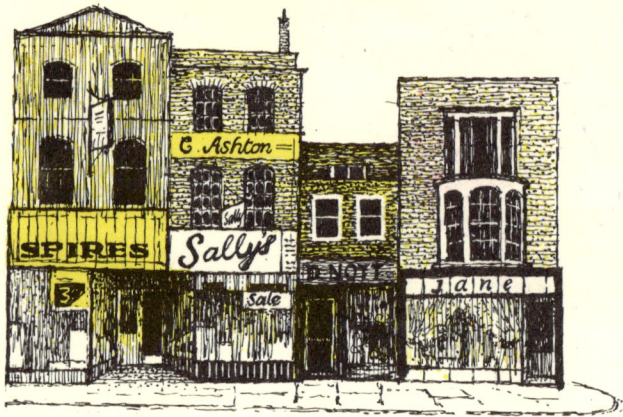

was a little, tiny, slip of a shop between two big ones. She could not see anyone inside. When she pushed the door it would not open. Then she saw a notice which said:

CLOSED
DINNER HOUR
1–2

"Oh dear!" said Penny. "The Clock Man must still be having his dinner. I will do my shopping first and come back again later."

It was when she stooped to pick up the basket again that she saw something shining on the pavement. It was a bright new key, rather like the one that opened the front door of the new house.

"Somebody must have dropped it,"

said Penny. "I'll take it home and give it to Mum. She'll know what to do with it."

She picked up the key and put it in her mother's purse.

When she reached the Self Service Store, she went round the shelves with her wire basket, choosing what she wanted. She felt *just* like a mother with six children at home, all with measles.

As she put each thing in her basket she crossed it off the shopping list, just as her mother did.

When Penny had done every bit of her mother's shopping, she said to herself:

"Now I'll spend my pocket-money!"

She went up to a man in a white apron and said:

"Please, will you lift down a tin of

Wuffo Dog Food for me, because I
can't quite reach it."

The man lifted it down.

"And here is the free dog bowl that is
being given away with it this week.
Your puppy is going to be lucky!" he
said with a smile.

"Isn't he!" said Penny. "It's a lovely bowl!"

It had DOG written on it in big black letters. And because he seemed a friendly man she said: "Please can you tell me when I shall hear the cuckoo? I've waited for so long."

The man seemed rather surprised, but he said:

"The cuckoo? Bless you, you won't ever hear the cuckoo here in the town. Only in the country!"

"Not ever?" asked Penny anxiously.

"Well, I've never heard one," said the man. He turned away to help someone else.

"Never hear the cuckoo here at all!" said Penny to herself. She could hardly believe it. "Everything seems to go wrong about my puppy!"

She had stopped pretending to be a mother with six children at home with measles. She was just Penny feeling very miserable, standing in the queue for the check-out.

"Cheer up, ducks!" said the girl sitting at the till. The ten-shilling note Penny handed her had several tear splodges on it.

Penny struggled out of the shop with her shopping basket. It was rather heavy. It bumped against her legs but she was too unhappy to care.

She had quite forgotten about the alarm clock. If there had not been a knot of people outside the little shop she might have walked straight past. She stopped to see what was happening. A little old man was standing by the door.

"I can't think what I can have done with it," he kept saying. "What a nuisance! It means I can't get into the shop unless I break the lock!"

"You had better put a new lock on the door, in case someone has picked up the key. They might try to get in and

steal some of your clocks," someone said.

Penny went very red. She pushed her way through and said to the old man:

"Please, I picked up a key on the pavement on my way to the Self Service Store. Is it yours?"

She took the key out of the purse and held it up. The old man peered at it through his spectacles. There was a buzz of talk in the little group of people.

"Why, bless me!" he said. "That's it! That's my key. Thank you very much, my dear. I'm very grateful to you."

He turned and fitted it into the lock and the little door opened at once. The people watching drifted away.

"Come inside, my dear, so that I can thank you properly," said the Clock Man. He closed the door behind her.

Penny looked round. There were clocks everywhere; on the little counter and hanging all over the walls, big clocks and little clocks. The big ones went "tick-tock", very loud and slow, and the little clocks went "tick-tick-tick" very quickly and quietly. The air was full of their ticking.

"Please," said Penny, "will you mend Daddy's alarm clock. He was late for work yesterday."

"Dear me!" said the Clock Man. "We can't have that happening. Let me see."

He switched on a bright little light, unscrewed the back of the clock and peered at the works through a magnifying glass, which he squeezed into one eye.

While he did this Penny stood and listened to the clocks ticking, and instead of saying, "tick-tock, tick-tock," they seemed to be saying, "Go-on! Go-on!"

Her face went redder and redder, and at last she said:

"Please, I wasn't going to open your door and steal your clocks. I was keeping the key to give to Mum because I knew she'd know what to do with it."

The old man looked up and smiled kindly at her.

"I'm quite sure you wouldn't steal anything, my dear. I'm very grateful to you for finding my key. Why, whatever's this? Have you been crying?"

Penny nodded miserably. Her face

just showed above the counter and he could see the smears on her cheeks.

"Won't you tell me what's the matter? You helped me. P'r'aps I can help you."

"I don't think anybody can help me," said Penny with a sniff. "It's because there aren't any cuckoos here, ever. The Self Service man said so."

"Dear, dear! And do you so specially want to hear a cuckoo?" said the Clock Man.

"Daddy said I couldn't have my puppy until the Spring came and I heard one, and I have tried to be good, and I haven't bothered him about it once. I've kept my old dressing-gown for a comfy bed for him, and I saved up for a tin of Wuffo, and I've got a bowl with DOG on it, and now it's all no good!"

"I shouldn't be so sure of that," said the Clock Man. "There's one kind of town cuckoo that the Self Service man may not know about, but I do!"

"Is there really?" said Penny, cheering up at once.

"Now you go on being patient, and good, and not bothering for just a bit longer. You never know what may happen! Now then, about this alarm clock. I don't think there is much wrong with it. You give me your Dad's name and address and I'll mend it and bring it round one evening this week."

So Penny told the Clock Man where she lived and then she said goodbye.

"And don't forget to go on listening for that cuckoo! You never know your luck!"

It was just one week later that Penny said to the King and Queen as she washed herself before breakfast:

"Do you know, your Majesties, I thought I heard the cuckoo in the night. But birds only sing in the daytime so I must have dreamed it."

When she was eating her boiled egg at breakfast, she told her father and mother as well.

"That's funny! I thought I heard a cuckoo too!" said her father. There was

a twinkle in his eye. "Have you noticed
something, Tuppence?"

"The Clock Man came round last
night with Daddy's mended alarm
clock. He brought a present for you!"
said her mother.

"For me?" said Penny.

"He said he was so grateful to you
for finding his key that he wanted you
to have a special clock of your very own.

It's one that somebody brought to be mended years and years ago. They never came to fetch it."

"There it is, hanging on the wall!" said her father. "You'd better go and look at it. It's getting late. I must hurry."

Penny rushed to look at the clock. It was more like a little wooden house than a clock. It had two chains hanging down from its works, each with a weight on the end, shaped like a fir cone. The hands of the clock were just pointing to eight o'clock. Above the white numbers, underneath the little roof, there was a tiny door. As Penny watched, there was a whirring noise inside the clock. The tiny door opened and out came a little wooden bird! It sang "Cuckoo!" eight times over because it was eight o'clock, and every

time it sang "Cuckoo!" it flapped its
wooden wings and nodded its head at
Penny. As soon as it had finished it went
back into its little house, and the tiny
door closed with a click.

"Will it come again?" said Penny.

"Every hour if you wind it properly,"
said her mother.

"And my puppy? Can I have it, now
we've all heard the cuckoo?" asked
Penny breathlessly.

"You shall have it this very day!" said Daddy.

And she did. And he was brown, with floppy paws, and there could not have been a better name for him than Bounce!